Ella spent her vacation on the farm where her cousin Grace lived. Grace had a pony called Toffee. He was called Toffee because his hair was the color of toffee candy. His ears twitched happily when he ate apples from Ella's hand.

Grace and Ella brushed Toffee's coat together. They fed him special food, like oats and beets.

"Can I have a pony?" Ella asked her parents back in the city.

"We can't keep a pony in our apartment," Dad said. "A pony needs lots of space."

"Your father is right," said Mom.

Ella missed Toffee, and she was sad that she couldn't have a pony.

At breakfast Ella said, "If we moved
to the country, I could have a pony!"

"How would I get to work on time?"
Mom asked.

"How about finding a pet that will fit
in our apartment?" Dad asked.

Ella knew her parents were right.
She was excited about choosing a pet.

The next Saturday morning, Ella asked,
"Can we go to the pet store today?"
"Of course we can," said Mom and Dad.

That afternoon, they took the bus to the biggest pet store in town.

"What cute puppies!" said Ella.

"Our apartment is too small for a dog," said Mom firmly.

There were a hundred different kinds
of pets. Ella looked at kittens, frogs, turtles,
birds, goldfish, rabbits, and even mice!

There were so many animals that Ella didn't know which pet to choose. She needed a small pet, but which animal would be best?

The birds were all chirping and
squawking. Over the noise, she heard
a short song. Which bird was singing?

She turned around and saw a bright
yellow canary. He started his song again,
and Ella thought he was singing just for her.
Finally, Ella knew which pet she wanted.

Ella carried the canary home in a new cage, and the other children on the bus stared.

"I'm going to call him Sunny because he's yellow like the sun," said Ella happily.

At home, Dad hung Sunny's cage up
in the living room.

"Listen to him sing!" said Mom.

"I think Sunny will fit in just fine!"
said Ella.

Think Critically

1. Why did Ella feel sad at the beginning of the story?

2. What happened in the middle of the story?

3. Why did Ella name her canary Sunny?

4. Why did Ella get a bird for a pet?

5. Do you think a canary is a good pet for an apartment? Why or why not?

 **Social Studies**

Make a Chart Make a chart with the heads *In the Country* and *In the City*. Write three animals that would be better kept in the country and three animals that would do well in the city.

School-Home Connection Tell a family member about the story. Then talk about animals that could be kept as pets in your home.